The Search for Big Lou

Lane Walker

The Fishing Chronicles
www.lanewalkerbooks.com

The Search for Big Lou by Lane Walker
Copyright © 2021 Lane Walker

ISBN 978-1-955657-11-2

For Worldwide Distribution
Printed in the U.S.A.

Published by Bakken Books
2021
www.lanewalkerbooks.com

Hometown Hunters
The Legend of the Ghost Buck
The Hunt for Scarface
Terror on Deadwood Lake
The Boss on Redemption Road
The Day It Rained Ducks
The Lost Deer Camp

The Fishing Chronicles
Monster of Farallon Islands
The River King
The Ice Queen
The Bass Factory
The Search for Big Lou

For more books, check out:
www.lanewalkerbooks.com

-1-

"I thought summer camp was supposed to be fun..." questioned Presley.

"We have to beat those knucklehead boys from B Cabin; we just have to!" exclaimed Ann.

Our whole summer hinged on one last competition at Camp Golden Arrow.

To add even more pressure, the winner of the notorious golden arrow trophy hadn't been won by a girl cabin in over ten years. The boys seemed to dominate the past decade, and they took great pride in the fact they were the annual winners.

"Two weeks ago, no one thought we stood a chance; every counselor would have picked our cabin to finish last," said Mia.

"Not all of them. Miss Katie was always in our corner; she knew we could do it," said Presley.

"True, but do you really think she thought we could? Or was she just trying to make us learn another Camp Golden Arrow lesson?" Ann said thoughtfully.

We all laughed.

Miss Katie surely did love giving us quotes and motivating our cabin, but deep down I knew without a shadow of a doubt that she believed in us.

"Girls, let's be honest though. How are we going to win? We are too far behind in points; it would take a miracle to pull this off," said Ann.

A miracle...

That was what I hoped would happen when I came to Camp Golden Arrow.

School had just wrapped up, and summer vacation was here. I was so excited when my mom said they had a surprise for me—until I found out the surprise. My emotions quickly turned to anger when she told me the surprise was two weeks—

fourteen whole days in the Mississippi wilderness at some teen summer camp.

No cell phones, no social media and none of my friends.

The thought of not having my cell phone was terrifying. I spent a lot of time on my phone, either texting or on social media, posting or scrolling through pictures. Not only did it serve as a great way to pass the time, I also was more outgoing with my phone than I was in person.

I was quiet and shy with few real friends. I lived in Hattiesburg, Mississippi. The city had a population of over 45,000 people. I liked living in a big city; it seemed easier to go unnoticed...to do my own thing. It wasn't that I didn't want friends; I just really didn't know how to find them.

As the old yellow bus chugged down the gravel dirt roads in route to Camp Golden Arrow, my mind raced. Where in the world is this place? I had never been on a trip with so many twists and turns. For the past two hours, it seemed like all I had seen was gravel and trees. I had officially lost all cell phone signal, and we still weren't even to camp yet.

I caught my reflection in one off the bus windows and quickly turned away. I hated what I saw.

The camp bus smelled of old mothballs and sweaty teenagers. The seats were worn and tattered, and every bump we hit on the road felt like an awkward punch to my legs.

Why does my mom hate me?

"Could this possibly get any worse?" I asked myself.

I had no idea what was in store for this 14-year-old city girl over the next two weeks.

-2-

Camp Golden Arrow had been established in 1914 by a group of churches from all over Mississippi. Lou Beaumont was one of the original founders and financial supporter of camp. Lou spent some time playing minor league baseball before starting a shipping and transportation company in Jackson, Mississippi. The company prospered, and Lou was a millionaire by the time he turned 40 years old.

He had grown up in the woods and on the water; he loved the outdoors. Lou often told clients that the outdoors kept him balanced and happy. If he wasn't at work, Lou could be found hunting or fishing on his land in Mississippi.

When the local members of his church came to him about an idea of starting a camp devoted to kids aged 8-16, Lou jumped on board, serving as the camp CEO and main financial backer. He donated $500,000 towards the purchase of 500 acres of pristine wilderness off Highway 53. Four large lakes fed by the Wolf River added to the attractiveness of the property. The largest of the lakes was David Lake.

Legend goes that after meeting with the real estate agent and negotiating a good price, Lou had one more test before agreeing to buy the acreage. He walked over to the trunk of his car and pulled out an old bamboo fishing pole.

"I like what I see...I really do," Lou said. "But if the fishing isn't good, I will find a different piece of land. Kids need to be able to feel the pride and adrenaline of reeling in a big fish!" he said.

Walking over towards some rocks, Lou flipped over several small stones before finding a huge night crawler.

With keen precision, Lou baited the hook and sent the line out about twenty feet offshore.

The real estate agent stood frozen, praying a fish would strike the worm. The deal was sure to bring a big commission check and some bragging rights for the agent.

It didn't take long before the tip of Lou's pole started dancing from a fish bite. He waited and jerked the rod setting the hook. He reeled in the fish and held it up for all to see.

It was a gorgeous, giant blue catfish.

The agent was thrilled.

"That's a big one, Lou—big one!" exclaimed the agent, knowing the fish had just sealed the deal for the sale.

Lou stopped and turned back to the agent.

"Big Lou, I like that. I like that a lot," Lou said.

From that time on, everyone called Lou Beaumont "Big Lou."

Luckily, Big Lou's pocketbook was as loud and boisterous as the businessman.

That summer construction had started, and by the end of the season, Camp Golden Arrow was built. Lou talked the committee into naming the camp after his favorite hunting arrow. He had a lot of luck with this one particular arrow that was golden in color.

The camp started out with eight cabins, a lunchroom, a church and a meeting center. A big house was also built near David Lake overlooking the camp. That house was for Big Lou.

And for the next forty years, Big Lou served as Camp Director and never missed a camp. His wife Lorna and all of Big Lou's kids spent their summers at Camp Golden Arrow. Big Lou was a proud dad of three girls.

After Big Lou's death, his son-in law, Norman Creed, took the reins as camp director.

Every summer the camp is sold out, hosting 200 kids for two-week stays, with over 1,600 kids attending different sessions throughout the summer. The bus ride was long—very long. The humming of the bus engine and wheels almost put me to sleep. My trance-like daze was interrupted by the screeching bus brakes. The driver took a tight right, turning onto what appeared to be a two-track trail. It definitely wasn't a road or a place where my parents would have ever chosen to drive their car.

We continued driving for five more minutes, navigating through washouts and deep potholes before the outline of an opening appeared on the horizon. The pine tree-lined trail gave way to a huge open field. In the distance were cabins and buildings...and tons of kids.

Camp Golden Arrow looked like its own small town nestled deep in the woods.

-3-

The bus I rode on wasn't full, but there were a lot of kids on it. Thankfully, I had my own seat near the front of the bus.

I didn't know a single person on the bus. My mom had driven me to a local church in Hattiesburg to board the bus to camp.

My parents both thought the summer camp was a good idea. My mom had attended it when she was younger and always talked about all the fun she had. She still is close to one of the girls she bunked with at Camp Golden Arrow.

Summer camp is supposed to be fun—something a kid looks forward to. Not to me, summer camp was a punishment. Two weeks before camp,

I had broken several of my parents' rules on my cell phone. I was allowed two hours a day of phone usage, and I had gotten caught twice in the same week pushing seven hours a day.

While that seemed like a lot to my parents, it didn't to me. They were convinced I was addicted to my cell phone. I told myself they just didn't know what it was like to be 14 years old.

"We are here! Get ready for the best summer of your lives!" yelled the bus driver. Kids started grabbing their suitcases and sleeping bags. You could tell the ones who were returning to camp; they were excited. Spotting all the new campers was also easy; they were much more reluctant to get off the bus. I knew I wasn't the only one who was nervous.

I stepped off the bus and was instantly greeted by mosquitoes and small flying bugs. I started freaking out, swatting in all directions.

"Honey, I wouldn't waste your energy. Those bugs live here, and you are just visiting," yelled the bus driver before shutting the door. Within seconds, the big yellow bus was kicking up a dust storm heading back towards civilization.

I stood there alone and scared.

After a couple awkward minutes, I heard a soft, comforting voice above all the other noise.

"Hey! Hey girl in the pink shirt! Can I help you?" asked the voice.

I turned to see a young, 20-something girl walking in my direction.

"Me?" I timidly asked.

"Yeah, let me help you. I remember my first year at camp; it's scary. What's your name?" she asked.

"Presley," I answered.

"Well, Presley, welcome to the greatest summer camp east of the Mississippi. My name is Katie; the campers call me Miss Katie," she said.

The girl was peppy, loud, and most of all, happy. I already didn't like her.

-4-

This place seemed more like a zoo than a summer camp. It was loud, and there was activity everywhere.

Behind me, a group of kids were throwing footballs and chasing each other. The basketball courts were full, and some of the older boys were in a competitive 5-on-5 game.

As we turned towards the main lodge, a breathtaking view of Lake David appeared. The sun was shining bright on the blue waters, giving it a brilliant sheen.

Lake David was a huge lake that bordered the back of Camp Golden Arrow. There were docks, kayaks, ziplines and a huge floating raft.

I loved the water, so the sight of Lake David was a welcome sight.

"You will love the lake; it's amazing and so much fun," offered Katie.

She added, "Do you like to fish?"

"Fish? Like hooks-and-bobbers fish?" I asked.

"Yeah, like fishing. Do you like it?" Katie asked.

"I don't dislike it," I said.

Katie stopped and looked intently at me. "Have you ever been fishing?" she asked.

"No," I said.

"Have you ever been kayaking?" she asked.

"No," I said, embarrassed.

I lived in the city. I did city things, I didn't want to say it out loud, but all this country stuff was new and frightening.

"You are going to have an epic 14 days at Camp Golden Arrow," reaffirmed Miss Katie.

I followed Miss Katie as we walked into the main registration building where tables were set up. She guided me to the S–Z table since my last name was Walton. "Here you go, Presley. They will take good care of you from here," she said.

She took two steps and turned back to the table. "What cabin is she in?" she asked the woman behind the table.

"Looks like she is D Cabin," the lady said.

A smirk filled Katie's face.

"Perfect, that means I will be your cabin counselor, Presley," she said, whirling around and disappearing into the crowd of campers.

"This just keeps getting better and better," I said to myself.

Once I was registered, the lady gave me a map and circled D Cabin.

"You lucked out, Presley! Your cabin has the best view!" she exclaimed, pointing out that D Cabin bordered Lake David. In fact, the back door of the cabin was just a few feet away from the lakeshore.

I left and walked toward the cabin, following the detailed map. As I passed several other cabins,

I guessed there had to be around 20 cabins total on each side of the lane.

Each one had a sizable letter burned into the wood at the top, so finding D Cabin was easy. I walked closer towards Lake David. The wooden screen door creaked and moaned as I tried to open it. It was heavy and caused me to drop my sleeping bag in the sand.

"Can I help you with that?" asked a gentle voice.

"Sure," I replied, looking up to see a slender black-haired girl standing in the doorway.

She opened the door and grabbed my sleeping bag out of the sand. As I stepped into the cabin,

-5-

As soon as I entered the cabin, my blood raced and my stomach began flip-flopping in uncomfortable knots.

The cabin, which was already full of girls and personalities, was loud and intimidating. Beyond them, I saw four sets of bunk beds. Six of the beds already had bags on them. I sheepishly followed Mia towards the back of the cabin towards one of the open ones.

"Thanks for the help," I mumbled.

"No problem. My name is Mia," she added.

My body was tense as I dropped my suitcase and sleeping bag on the only available bed left.

The cabin was full. I was the last one to arrive.

"Looks like we are bunkmates," Mia said, gesturing towards the top bunk above me.

I just smiled. I didn't know what to say or how to act. I thought this whole idea of spending two weeks at summer camp with people I didn't know very strange. The other girls in the cabin went back to their own stuff without paying me another look. They had already made their own groups.

I was used to being overlooked. Back home, all the girls seemed to have a clique or a group to hang out with.

That wasn't the case for me; I was a loner. I used to tell myself it was by choice, but it really wasn't. The truth was I became extremely uncomfortable around groups of people and often just kept to myself.

How would I do that here?

The small cabin left little space to hide. As I unpacked, I found myself reaching for my cell phone.

No signal—nothing. I shut off the phone and shoved it deep into my suitcase. It meant I wouldn't be able to access my parents or any social media. I had trouble going ten minutes—let alone two weeks without being on my phone.

I unpacked and sat on my bed.

Now what? I thought to myself.

After a couple minutes, I felt the bottom bunk jerk and creak as Mia jumped down to the floor.

"Do you want to meet Ann?" she asked.

I looked around the room.

Mia could tell I was trying to figure out who Ann was.

"Oh, she's not in here; she's out back," she explained.

I followed Mia out the back door of D Cabin. The view of the lake stopped me as I admired the sheer size and light-blue water tones.

I looked to my left and could make out a small silhouette sitting down on the lakeshore with a fishing pole.

"Hey, Ann, this is Presley. She is going to bunk by us in our cabin," said Mia loudly.

Ann turned and smiled. Gummy worms and licorice fell out of her pocket when she turned.

"Ann doesn't talk much, but she is really funny once you get to know her. Oh, and she loves candy—anything with sugar," said Mia.

After Ann turned around, I nearly passed out. I thought I was in some strange sci-fi movie.

Ann was an exact clone to Mia; they were identical twins!

I had a math class with a set of twins back in Hattiesburg, but they looked different. One had a large mole by her left ear, making them easy to tell apart.

But not Mia and Ann. They couldn't have looked more like each other. Their hair, skin tone, and even the way they smiled was identical.

-6-

The three of us stood by the lake as Ann fished. The girl may have been quiet, but she could fish. She caught two or three big bass as we sat and talked. It was the first time I had ever been that close to a fish that wasn't in an aquarium. Fishing looked pretty cool. Mia was easy to talk to, and Ann seemed to like listening more than talking.

From the beginning, the twins seemed different. I didn't feel like everything I said or did was being judged.

The twins were just nice—really nice. They told me about their farm and how they loved to show horses.

I was fascinated with life on a farm. I had never

been to one before, but I had seen several on the ride to camp. They looked interesting and peaceful.

Our conversation was interrupted when a loud, booming familiar voice bellowed, "Ladies of D Cabin, let's go!"

We turned to see Miss Katie with her head out the back door, motioning for us to return to the cabin.

Ann quickly reeled in her fishing line and sat the pole down behind us near a log bench.

Miss Katie was one of the loudest, most passionate people I had ever met. It was evident she loved life and working at the camp.

"Girls, you are about to embark on the greatest summer adventure of your life. In the next two weeks, you will make lifelong, lasting memories. You are valued, and you matter at Camp Golden Arrow," she said.

She had my attention; something was authentic and genuine in her voice.

"Okay, how many girls have ever been to this camp?" she asked.

Five of the eight girls raised their hands.

Mia, Ann and I were the only ones who weren't returning campers which made sense why the other girls were so connected with each other.

"Ladies, let me tell you something. This is the year that D Cabin claims the golden arrow trophy!" declared Miss Katie.

Snickers and laughter started to fill the cabin.

"Miss Katie, sorry to burst your bubble. But you know that no girl cabin has won the golden trophy in the past ten years," said a tall, gangly girl with a blue baseball cap.

Another girl added, "Plus, the boys from B Cabin have won it the last two years."

She quickly added, "Marshall Lawrence would never lose to a bunch of girls."

-7-

Marshall Lawrence was known as "Marsh" around Camp Golden Arrow. Marsh was tall and muscular; he was really big for his age. Even though he was only 14 years old, Marsh was already 6'3" and a super athlete. Rumors swirled that he was already having professional baseball scouts watching his games. All the boy campers looked up to him, and the girls thought he was cute.

He was the all-American boy, and no one knew that more than Marsh.

"How in the world are we going to win the golden arrow trophy?" asked a girl who was resting on her cot. "There is no way we can beat the boys from B Cabin in the tournament events."

"Sorry to interrupt…but could someone please explain to me what the golden arrow trophy is," I said.

The returning campers turned and looked at me in disgust.

"It's only the biggest deal at camp," said one of the girls.

Miss Katie quickly shot the girl a stern look.

"Easy, these girls are new. How would they possibly know?" asked Miss Katie.

"Winning the golden arrow trophy is legendary at camp. Since its existence, only two girl cabins have ever won," said Miss Katie.

She went on to explain the history of the award. "The competition, which had been established over thirty years ago, takes place the last week of camp. Each cabin competes in a variety of events, with each event collecting points. Whatever cabin accumulates the most points at the end of the week is presented the golden arrow trophy.

"The first-place winner of each event is awarded

ten points, second place receives eight points and third place earns five points.

"The fishing tournament, the most anticipated event, is held on the last day. The cabin that catches the biggest overall fish receives ten points plus an extra five-point bonus.

"Each person in the winning cabin receives a Camp Golden Arrow champion t-shirt. The credibility that comes with winning the golden arrow trophy is the most important part of winning. Other campers talk about the past champions like they had the won the Super Bowl or something.

"To say it was a big deal to win the contest would be a huge understatement."

The whole contest seemed silly to me; I wasn't super competitive.

"Have any girl cabins ever close to winning?" I asked.

"Not really," said Miss Katie.

But she quickly added, "But that doesn't mean this can't be the year—our year!"

The other girls laughed and went back to organizing their bunks.

"Wait!" yelled out one of the girls. She added, "We could always just catch Big Lou!"

Laughter erupted even louder, and even Miss Katie laughed out loud when she heard that suggestion.

-8-

The search for Big Lou had become a summer camp tall tale the past decade. Stories were told around the lunch tables and campfires about Big Lou.

It all started innocently ten years ago during a cold, spring day at Camp Golden Arrow. One of the college counselors was working with the State Department of Natural Resources to plant blue catfish across the state of Mississippi. During the fish-planting process, the counselor came across a gigantic blue catfish. The fish had a head like a tank and weighed close to 70 pounds. They had netted the fish in Wolf Creek, which was only a couple miles away from Camp Golden Arrow.

He had pleaded with the conservation officer to let him put the gigantic catfish at the camp in Lake David. He knew this catfish had the potential to break 100 pounds. He knew that planting a fish of that size with those genetics would make Lake David even more popular. It would also add even more excitement for campers at Camp Golden Arrow.

The counselor decided to nickname the fish "Big Lou" after Lou Beaumont, the founding father of Camp Golden Arrow.

The story is told that he released the fish near the docks of Camp Golden Arrow. That summer, the camp director announced that anyone who caught Big Lou would receive a bonus 40 points for their cabin towards the golden arrow award. Everyone set out that summer to hook Big Lou, but no one did, In fact, no one has ever hooked the fish since.

Ten years of campers' dreams and hopes, but no one had ever hooked the fish. Every year, the legend seemed to grow with stories of campers seeing a big dark shadow or catching a glimpse of Big Lou. There were so many stories, but most were made up. Some could have been true but telling the factual ones from the fake ones was hard. Multiple Big Lou sightings were reported each year, but no one put much stock into them.

"So, basically, if someone catches that fish, her cabin could win the golden arrow trophy. That could be the way we beat the boys," said Miss Katie with determination.

"Ten years and no one has ever seen or caught Big Lou—seems hopeless to me," mumbled one of the girls.

"Nothing is impossible," stated Ann optimistically.

All the girls stopped and stared at Ann. It was the first time she had said something in front of the large group.

"That's right! That's the spirit!" exclaimed Miss Katie.

The cabin went silent; no one had expected Ann to say something.

Right then, a low, strange sound caught my attention. At first, I thought it was someone's watch; then the noise started to get louder.

I turned to Mia and whispered, "Do you hear that sound?"

She nodded as we walked towards the noise, which happened to be coming from my bottom bunk.

"Girls, what is that noise?" asked Miss Katie.

The sound had become so loud the entire cabin had stopped talking and could hear it echoing in the old log cabin. By the time we had reached my sleeping bag, it was really loud.

It kind of reminded me of my cellphone vibrating loudly, but the sound was too loud for that.

I reached down and slowly pulled back the top layer of my sleeping bag.

Coiled up inside was a huge rattlesnake!

I was so startled that I stepped backward into

Mia. She tripped over me as the rest of the girls ran shrieking out of the cabin.

A huge, venomous rattlesnake was coiled in my bed, ready to strike.

-9-

I had learned from one of my science teachers at school that the body reacts in a stressful situation in one of three ways: fight, flight or freeze.

Once I had taken the initial step backward into Ann, mine had then decided to freeze; I was as stiff as a board.

I stared at the snake as the rattle hiss grew louder and louder. Then something strange happened. The shaking sound of the rattle was suddenly silenced by a loud explosion of laughter coming from the back of the cabin. I turned to see three boys hysterically laughing and pointing as they stood in the doorway.

Standing in the doorway were some of the B

Cabin boys. I knew right away the boy in front was Marsh. The girls in the tent had described every detail about him—even his flowing blond hair.

I jumped up and grabbed the snake, whipping it at the boy. I knew now that the snake was only a realistic toy put there to scare the girls—to prank us. Our cabin was the first to be pranked by the boys of B Cabin, and it wouldn't be the last. Marsh had a reputation for pranking and pushing the limits at Camp Golden Arrow. We simply happened to be his first victims at this year's camp.

Miss Katie stormed back in, but the boys were already gone.

"Well, girls, it seems like some boys think it's funny to scare people. Don't let those boys get to you. I will talk to their counselor; I know him personally," she promptly assured us.

The other girls were faking their laughter, trying to act like the snake antic had been a funny joke—like they weren't really scared. I think once they saw Marsh was involved, they wanted to look calm and cool. But for Ann, Mia and me, nothing was cool about Marsh and the B Cabin boys.

Ann walked back over, and the three of us went to our bunks.

The twins could tell I was furious, so they just sat with me in silence for several minutes.

Finally, Ann spoke up. "Don't worry, Presley."

"I am not worried," I snapped. My sharp response caught Ann off guard.

Mia quickly stepped in. "No, Presley, that is not what she means. What she is saying is we got your back. Trust me, we will get revenge on those boys from B Cabin," stated Mia confidently.

Revenge sounded good at the moment. "Revenge it is, girls," I softly said.

A sly grin materialized on Ann's face. "I have an idea that will put those boys of B Cabin in their place. They need to know they shouldn't mess with our cabin—well, at least the three of us," said Ann.

We scooted in closer as Ann whispered her devious plan.

As she described it in great detail, two thoughts ran through my mind. The first one was, how genius the prank was going to be. Ann was sharp; she had come up with the idea so fast. Then I wondered if this wasn't the first time Ann and Mia had pranked someone.

The second part of the plan turned my happiness into concern. The second question was a more critical question. *Are there certain rules or guidelines where they can throw us out of camp?*

It didn't matter, her plan would get us revenge, and I wasn't sold on Camp Golden Arrow anyway.

-10-

The rest of the day we walked around the campgrounds, getting to know where everything was and becoming familiar with the layout.

Camp Golden Arrow was literally set up like its own real town. Over the years, the property had really grown, and everything from a snack shack, gift shop, meeting rooms and an auditorium had been added. Ann told us she planned on hitting the snack shack every day and hoped they had enough candy in stock for the next two weeks.

I felt a positive, happy vibe as we walked and talked. Every once in a while, I would feel around in my back pocket. At first my heart would race, then I remembered I didn't have my phone. I was shocked at how many times I kept reaching for it. I was slowly starting to not miss it.

The twins were easy to talk to.

As we walked, we talked about Ann's plan to get back at the B Cabin boys, especially Marsh.

It was brilliant! If we could pull this off, these boys, or anyone else in camp, for that matter, would never mess with us again.

The first night always began with the back-to-camp bonfire and fun activities. A lot of cool stuff and wacky contests take place at the outside theater in the middle of the camp. The area is wide open around the huge campfire, and each camper brings his or her own chairs or blankets to sit on. The counselors perform funny skits and karaoke on the permanently fixed wooden stage. The very last activity is an old-fashioned campfire ghost story.

Other campers told us all about it and how it freaks them out, making the walk back to the cabin even spookier. They made it sound like being scared was something fun—like a camp ritual. Personally, I didn't like being scared.

The three of us sat and watched the program, and it was fantastic! Miss Katie was hilarious in her skit, and the counselors seemed cool. The entire evening happening was well done. Obviously, they had put a lot of time into planning the event. The last event was a dramatic, scary story by a camp worker. He wore overalls and an old, faded Camp Golden Arrow hat. I had seen the man a couple times earlier in the day. I thought he was the same guy who was on the tractor fixing some posts by the baseball field when I got off the camp bus.

When he started talking, the entire camp fell silent. His voice changed as he told this creepy story about some guy who was missing a hand; the guy had a hook or something. But the way he told it made it even more frightening. His voice would change with each character and had dramatic pauses.

It was one of the most engaging stories I had ever heard. It took place on the railroad near a river, and how this man came back each Halloween looking for his lost hand.

And even though I knew it was just a story, the telling of it made the hair on the back of my neck stand stiff. Mia slid closer to Ann and me as the story unfolded.

When the story ended, all the campers cheered, but I sensed a nervous buzz among the campers. Most tried to laugh it off and make fun of it, but I could tell they were actually scared. Afterwards, campers had 30 minutes to linger before mandatory lights out in the cabins. Everyone seemed nervous to walk back to their cabin.

The mood was perfect for our plan.

I spotted Marshall and the B Cabin boys showing off for some of the female camp counselors up near the stage. They were being really loud in their attempt to impress them.

"It's time," I said to Ann and Mia.

The three of us slipped back quietly to our cabin.
It was time to payback the boys from snake prank.
Marsh had no idea what was about to happen.

-11-

When we got back to our cabin, we went to work. Mia reached into her suitcase and pulled out a small overnight bag. Then she pulled out a tube of sunscreen. Mia and Ann went to the nearby mirror and started applying the sunscreen all over their face. I went to the table and grabbed two flashlights. I clicked both of them on to make sure they had working batteries.

I handed each girl a light and stood amazed as they clicked them on. The dim flashlight gave the creamy, white lotion a ghostly look. *Perfect!* They pulled up the hoods on their black-hooded sweatshirts as we crept out the back door of the cabin.

Marsh has no idea what's coming.

I headed back to the outside amphitheater, and the B Cabin boys were still strutting around showing off. I walked over to stand near Marsh, hoping to get his attention. Mia and Ann stayed back in the shadows behind one of the cabins.

After a couple minutes, he stopped when he noticed me standing behind him.

"What you want?" he asked.

"Nothing, I just wanted to warn you that you really hurt my friends' feelings with your little snake prank."

"Yeah, so…" Marsh responded.

"Well, I just wanted to let you know that she was pretty shook up. She was looking for you," I said.

"Oh, scary! Your little girl friend knows where to find me," he said, laughing as he turned back to his friends.

"Okay," I said with a smirk as I walked away.

My response caught his attention but only for a second.

Ann was stationed near the snack shack, sitting alone on the front porch.

I snuck into the small cabin adjacent to the amphitheater where the camp microphone and speaker was. Then I drew a deep, low voice and said, "Excuse me, but I wanted to announce the winner of our free banana float is from B Cabin. Marshall Lawrence, please come to the snack shack and claim your prize."

I peeked out of the cabin and could see Marsh high-fiving all his buddies and making gestures as he started to walk towards the snack shack alone.

After a couple of minutes he arrived, and Ann was sitting and staring at him as he approached.

"What are you doing?" he asked. He was startled with Ann's chalky appearance.

She lifted her head to stare at him in an awkward, creepy silence.

Even I have to admit she did look freaky.

"Hey, Freak, where's my banana split?" he asked again. Ann did nothing; she said just stared.

The awkward silence was broken by a loud horn which signaled campers had to return to their cabins for the night.

Marsh's voice trailed off and quaked slightly as he finally stammered, "Whatever…" I could tell he was still freaked out by the man's story. Now seeing a pale-faced girl staring silently at him with only the limited glow of her flashlight put him on edge.

As he walked towards his cabin, every couple of steps, he kept turning back to look at Ann.

She sat still staring at him on the front porch of the store.

Marsh turned the corner and walked toward his cabin, peeking back around the corner one more time to confirm that Ann was still sitting in the same spot.

She was.

But when he turned to walk up his cabin steps, perched on the front was the same girl he had just seen at the snack shop…or so he thought.

He knew there was no way she could have

gotten there in front of him. Stumbling back, he looked over his shoulder, confirming that she was still sitting on the store steps.

But sitting on the steps of his cabin was Ann. Well, at least he thought it was Ann. Mia sat there staring at him.

"What the…?! How did you get here?" he asked, stammering before stumbling back.

Mia said nothing and continued to stare.

Seeing the big, macho superstar scared out of his mind was hilarious.

Marsh turned back towards B Cabin, and Mia was gone. He started rubbing his eyes. When he turned back to the store, Ann was gone as well. But one thing was obvious, Marsh was confused and scared.

We giggled back in our cabin as the girls washed off their sunscreen. We had certainly gotten one over on the great Marshall Lawrence.

The next morning at breakfast I overheard some of the other boys from B Cabin talking. They said that Marsh didn't sleep at all last night. He seemed freaked out and kept getting up looking out the window towards the snack shop.

Identical twin friends come in handy, especially when there is a prank war.

-12-

The cafeteria door swung open, making a loud banging sound on the side of the wall. In staggered Marsh with a little less swagger to his step. He looked tired and exhausted. His face was pale, and his eyes squinted from the bright cafeteria lights.

He went through the breakfast line stumbling and out of sorts. It was obvious he hadn't slept.

He sat down with the other boys from his cabin. After a couple of minutes, Mia walked over and stood behind him. He turned.

"Hi, Marsh," she said in a low creepy voice.

"You!" He added, "Leave me alone, you freak!"

"No problem, I will leave you alone," said Mia as she walked over and stood by the exit door. Marsh just glared at her. He wasn't sure if he should be scared or continue to act cool.

A minute later, Ann walked over.

"Hi, Marsh," she said.

"I thought I told you to leave me alone!"

"What? That is so rude. This is the first time I have talked to you today," replied Ann.

She reached into her pocket, grabbed a handful of gummy worms, and put them on Marsh's plate. Then she walked over and stood next to Mia.

The three of us began laughing hysterically.

Marsh's face went from being scared to angry. He had no idea until that moment that Ann and Mia were identical twins.

By this time everyone in B Cabin figured out the prank. All but Marsh were laughing.

His once pale face was now a bright red. The girls of D Cabin had just gotten one over on the great Marshall Lawrence.

He didn't like it when he was the one people were laughing at.

We were the talk of the camp the rest of the day. When we got back to our cabin, the girls cheered. At least for a couple hours, we had gotten one over on Marsh.

That afternoon, the three of us went fishing off the boat dock. It was so much fun! I had never been fishing before. The first time I hooked into a bass, it fought and fought. I was so proud when I reeled it in. I could see why so many people liked to fish. The peaceful, calm waters were also intriguing to me.

It seemed like we didn't have a care in the world that afternoon. We caught a lot of fish, and Ann was an amazing fisherman. She cracked me up as she continually pulled sugary snacks from her pocket. It seemed like she had an endless supply of snacks.

Today's choice of candy was jawbreakers and licorice. She told us she had stocked up at the snack shop last night. She hoped she had enough candy to get her through the rest of the day.

The sun was starting to set, and the red-and-pink hues illuminated a different shade on the water. I was speechless at the pure beauty of being outside.

I was used to seeing concrete and buildings. I was surprised at how the beauty even captivated the twins. They saw this stuff every day on their farm, but it seemed like it was still something new whenever they were in the outdoors. They had a genuine appreciation for the wilderness.

Our tranquil fishing on the dock was interrupted when Miss Katie hollered our names from the back door of the cabin.

We reeled in our poles and walked back towards her. As we approached the open door, I could see the look of concern on Miss Katie's face.

Another man was also there. He looked more professional than Miss Kate—like he was someone important, and he didn't look happy.

-13-

"I take it you're the twins. Can you please take me to your bunks?" the man asked.

"That's mine, sir," Ann quickly said.

"I need you both to empty your pockets," said the man. The three of us were confused. No one in the cabin was with us but this man and Miss Katie.

Ann pulled out a handful of candy and wrappers. Mia had nothing in her pockets.

"I told you she was guilty," the man snapped to Miss Katie.

"Now hold on Mr. Creed, that doesn't make her guilty," said Miss Katie.

"Young lady, I will need you to empty your suitcase," said Mr. Creed.

I spoke up.

"What's going on? What is happening?" I asked.

"Just empty your suitcase to make him happy," Miss Katie said confidently. I could tell she didn't agree with Mr. Creed.

Ann reached under her bed and pulled up her suitcase. She laid it on the bed and unzipped it. Just as she was opening the top of her suitcase, candy started to fall out in all directions.

"Still think she's innocent?" Mr. Creed asked sharply.

"Ann, can you explain this?" asked Miss Katie.

Ann just stood staring at the candy. She was nervous and knew something wasn't right. The candy all had an orange price tag on it.

The colored price tag meant only one thing; it was candy from the camp store. Ann didn't know what to say. She hadn't been to the snack shop since yesterday and hadn't put any in her suitcase.

"Ann, I am going to need you to come with us," said Miss Katie.

"She didn't steal any candy," Mia shouted.

"We got a report from an anonymous camper that a young lady matching her description was seen stealing candy from the camp store this morning. We take theft quite seriously at Camp Golden Arrow," stated Mr. Creed.

"Wait! No way! We have been with her all day. She hasn't been to the store this entire day. The last time she was there was last night, and she didn't steal any candy," I said.

"Young lady, I need you to come with me," said Mr. Creed. The screen door on the cabin slammed, making an evil, pounding sound.

"This doesn't make any sense," I said turning to Mia.

The look on Mia's face was clear. She was angry; she knew exactly what was going on.

"Apparently our friend didn't learn his lesson the first time he messed with us. I think it's time we up the ante; no one messes with my sister," she said.

"Huh?" I replied, confused.

"It wasn't an anonymous source; it was Marsh. This is his way of paying us back for our prank," explained Mia.

-14-

"This isn't going to stand. Ann would never steal anything. We will make him pay for this," said Mia.

I heard a different tone in her voice—one that said she was going to protect her sister.

"What are we going to do now?" I asked. I had the strange feeling that things were starting to get out of hand. The prank war had started off as a fun way to pay back Marsh for the snake incident, but now the approach was different in tone and attitude.

"Do you think that's a good idea?" I asked. I figured Marsh would stop at nothing to be the best—the top dog. If we one-upped him, he would likely respond with something even more sinister.

"Let's go see where Ann is," Mia finally snorted.

We ran out the front door and watched as they escorted Ann into the main building—the same place where we had registered only yesterday.

We followed and sat on the front porch waiting.

After an hour, Ann finally appeared with Miss Katie. We both stood up.

"Girls, before you say anything, I know Ann didn't steal anything. Unfortunately, Mr. Creed is convinced she did. I managed to stop him from kicking her out of camp, but she has clean-up duty after lunch the rest of the week," said Miss Katie.

"For something she didn't do?!" snapped Mia.

"Mia, it's fine. It's nothing I can't handle," said Ann. She seemed calm and confident.

"We will help you!" I volunteered.

After lunch, we walked back into the kitchen and each grabbed an apron. We started picking up trash and plates in the cafeteria. A large group was still eating, as we tried to keep the floors clean.

I looked over my right shoulder and noticed someone had dropped his plate on the floor. Of course, it had to be hot dogs and baked beans for lunch. I swept up the ugly mess of yellow, red and brown, and walked over to the garbage to dump it.

"Excuse me, miss. You missed a spot," said a familiar voice. I turned to see more beans and other food lying in the exact same spot on the floor.

Marsh….

He found it funny to torture and embarrass us in the lunchroom. I turned to walk towards the mess, but Mia zoomed in and cleaned it up without missing a beat.

The B Cabin boys were laughing and joking. They found Marsh's antics hilarious. His revenge wasn't over yet, and I could tell that there was no limit to what he would do to win.

It was only the second day of camp, and I had managed to make friends and an enemy.

I liked the friends much better.

Marsh finally grew tired of dropping food and left the cafeteria. The other boys of B Cabin followed him around like little puppy dogs.

"It's time to pay him back," Mia said picking up and tying the trash bag.

"No, not this time," said Ann.

Stunned, both Mia and I turned to Ann. Her apron was covered in mustard and ketchup, but her chin was still held up high.

"Girls, we can keep playing this game over and over with Marsh. He won't stop until he wins every time. I think he will do whatever it takes to show us up," said Ann.

She added, "I think we need to enjoy camp. Marsh is trying to make it miserable, but there are so many fun things about camp."

I thought for a moment and was really proud of Ann. She had been accused of stealing and had to clean up the cafeteria as a result, but she was staying positive.

"So, Marsh is just going to get away with lying and getting you in trouble?" I asked.

"I didn't say that…" said Ann as her voice trailed off.

-15-

"Girls, we only have 12 days left at Camp Golden Arrow, and I want to enjoy them. But I have a plan for Marsh and the boys from B Cabin," said Ann.

"What are you thinking?" asked Mia.

"Marsh thinks he is so cool and has to win; he always has to be on top. So, these small pranks back and forth will just keep getting worse and worse. We need to hit the one thing that he will remember," said Ann.

Still confused, I asked, "What would that be?"

"We need to win the golden arrow trophy," she declared.

I laughed. I wasn't expecting that response.

"Didn't you hear Miss Katie say that no girl cabin has won in over ten years? Plus, B Cabin has won the last two years in a row. They are the clear favorites again this year," I said.

I added, "That seems impossible."

I was beginning to think maybe the mustard and ketchup fumes were playing games with Ann's head. But the more I thought about it, I knew she was right.

The golden arrow contest was the most prestigious award at camp and something that everyone talked about for years—not just for a day or two. Not only did the winning cabin get bragging rights and the trophy, they each got a golden arrow champion shirt.

The trophy would be nice, the shirt would be cool, but beating Marsh and the boys of B Cabin would be epic.

"Great thought, but that seems impossible," said Mia.

I questioned, "How in the world are we going to

beat those boys? We can't compete in those sports contests and would need to win some of them to even have a chance."

"Nothing is impossible." Ann repeated the phrase I had heard her say once before.

I knew she must have had some kind of plan. There was no way Ann would say something like that without having something in mind. But I knew our cabin wasn't capable of beating those boys. *We just aren't golden-arrow material.*

"You girls are thinking too small; there is an easy way to beat them," said Ann.

"Okay, I give in. How are we going to beat Marsh and B Cabin?" asked Mia.

"We are going to catch Big Lou," Ann answered confidently.

-16-

That night I struggled to sleep. Not being able to sleep at summer camp in a cabin of girls makes for a long night. I was tired and frustrated. In a way Marsh was seemingly getting away with everything. I was going to do my best to catch the famous fish, but realistically it seemed unlikely.

A trio of girls—one who had never fished before—catching one specific tagged fish that hasn't been caught in ten years. The lake was huge, the fish, if it was still alive, could be anywhere.

Not only that, but there would be well over 200 kids fishing the lake on the day of the fishing contest, and all of them dreamed about hooking into Big Lou.

I fluffed my pillow, thinking maybe that would help me fall asleep faster. When I sat up, I noticed the giant, white moon shining over the lake. The window out the back of our cabin almost drew the moon into Camp Golden Arrow.

I kept thinking about what Ann had said: "Nothing is impossible."

Two days ago, when my mom had told me how much fun I was going to have at camp and that I would meet some new real friends…that had seemed impossible as well.

But it wasn't—it was happening.

Mia and Ann were already closer than any friends I had back in Hattiesburg. The last thought I had before falling asleep was Big Lou's surfacing under the huge June moon above the lake. I pictured the fish enjoying the moon as much as I was—just waiting and counting down the days until one of us reeled him in.

The legend of Big Lou was the biggest legend at Camp Golden Arrow. The camp gift store even sold t-shirts with the image of Big Lou floating along the bottom of Lake David. I had seen tons of kids wearing the shirts with the huge catfish on the front around camp. The back had one simple phrase: "The Search for Big Lou" in big, bold black letters. I wondered if the fish even existed, or if the legend was just a marketing ploy to sell shirts at camp. The chance of hooking into Big Lou made the last day of camp even more exciting.

The morning sun shined in through the same window that had showcased the gorgeous moon from the previous night. Most campers didn't need alarm clocks at camp. In fact, I usually slept in until 10:00 a.m. when I was at home during the summer months. I closed all my blinds to make my room as dark as possible.

At camp, you couldn't do that. The sunrise woke us up early and signaled breakfast.

The cafeteria had a fresh breakfast of eggs, toast and sausage. I couldn't help but be thankful we weren't put on the cleanup crew for breakfast. The smell of eggs and the texture of grease made me want to throw up.

Sitting down, I sipped my orange juice slowly as I waited for my brain to wake up.

"Look at him sitting over there," noted Mia.

Turning to look over her shoulder, I could see Marsh a couple of tables away. His hair was combed to perfection; it was obvious he had gotten up early to put hair gel in it. I also noticed he was wearing his golden trophy winning gold t-shirt from the previous year.

I figured he wore it to remind other campers who the champion was.

"Better keep that one clean," I thought to myself. *He won't be getting one this year.*

-17-

Everyday camp life was very structured and busy. Our schedule was jampacked with nature lessons, summer events and activities. We spent the rest of the first week exploring and learning about some of the animals in the woods around Camp Golden Arrow.

I really enjoyed seeing a variety of animal footprints and wildlife. The thrill of the week was seeing a whitetail buck near a swamp on the north side of Lake David. The campers from our cabin had gone on a hiking exploration that lasted most of the day. We were far from camp when I noticed something moving in the nearby brush. I tried to edge closer when the bushes suddenly shook and out leaped a six-point buck. I had never seen one that close; it was awesome!

Some other highlights from the first week of camp included spending every minute with my new two best friends, Mia and Ann. We were close and had so much fun together. I just knew in my heart we would be friends for life after camp.

My mom was right; I loved camp! I started to realize that first week that a lot of my fear and anxiety had stopped me from enjoying certain parts of life—like friendships and late-night snacks, which Ann always provided. Even thought she had been accused of stealing from the store, she still went back to restock her supplies of licorice, gummy worms and other sugary candy.

Every day from 1:00–3:00 p.m. we had free time. Campers could swim, fish, shoot bows or make crafts. It was my favorite time of camp. Most days we fished or swam in the waters of Lake David. The beach, called Beaumont Beach after the founder of camp, was close to our cabin. The Mississippi summer days were so hot and muggy, and the cool lake water was refreshing. I also started to really enjoy fishing. We caught all kinds of fish around the lake. Fishing off the end of the boat dock was one of my favorite spots.

Miss Katie turned out to be super cool.

She apologized to Ann about the candy stealing episode. She knew she was innocent. We spent lots of time talking to her. She was a counselor who really made me feel like she cared.

Sunday, as we rested on our cots, we were in shock that seven days had passed. We were officially one week away from having to go home. When I first arrived at Camp Golden Arrow, I couldn't wait to leave. Not now. I wanted to stay forever.

"This week is going by even faster than the first one," said Mia.

"For sure, especially since tomorrow is the first day of the golden trophy competition. "

The seven-day event had exactly seven competitions with a different one each day.

Monday would be archery, Tuesday was kick-ball, Wednesday was swimming, Thursday was basketball, Friday was a two-mile run, Saturday was dodgeball, and Sunday was the fishing competition.

Our plan was simple; we had to win one of the events during the week and then catch Big Lou on Sunday. The rest would be history, and the girls of D Cabin would be famous forever. They would even talk about us just like Big Lou—as legends.

At least that was the plan…

-18-

Sunday night was one of the funniest nights of my life. Our cabin had our own campfire on the banks of Lake David. Everyone was in a good mood, and Miss Katie treated all of us to s'mores.

I had never had one before; they were the best-tasting treat ever! I loved cooking the marshmallow over the fire, sandwiching it with a piece of chocolate between two graham crackers. The hot marshmallow melts the chocolate bar, making a sticky, mouthwatering treat.

Miss Katie led us in songs, and the girls told funny stories. We stayed up well past midnight. The stars were more vibrant than ever and danced across the night sky. I was surrounded by friends and in love with camp life. That night I didn't have any trouble sleeping. I was content with myself for the first time in a long time.

Monday morning, the first official day of Camp Golden Arrow competition, was exciting. While I was no Robin Hood, I had enjoyed all the archery stations and learning to shoot a bow. Each cabin had a specific time to shoot, and ours was in the afternoon. Ann's lunchtime punishment had ended, and we had our lunch break time back.

The three of us had become close friends with the girls in the cabin next to us. Our group liked to play sand volleyball near the beach on Lake David. The court was full-size, and the sand was sugary white. It didn't match the darker beach sand from Lake David.

We were pretty good, making me wish that volleyball was one of the sports for the competition. If it had been one, we might have stood a chance at winning at least one event.

It was right before lunch, and we had been playing for the last half hour. Sally, our friend from C Cabin was serving. She had a bad hit, and the volleyball went into the lake. I walked over trying to grab the ball before it floated out farther into the lake. That was our only volleyball, and our game was too good not to finish.

When I first entered the water, I tiptoed in as the cold water shocked my feet. The ball had floated out about ten feet in the water and hung in the low waves.

As I walked towards the ball, the lake water rushed over my lower torso. I reached as far as I could, gripping the volleyball just enough to bring it in. The other girls were teasing me to hurry up as I squeezed the ball and brought it closer to my chest. I turned and started walking towards the shore. I had taken two steps when I noticed a big dust cloud in the water in front of me.

I stood still, squinting into the water to see what I had scared up. I figured it was a small bass or maybe a painted turtle.

The cool water was soothing on my sunburnt legs, so I waited a couple extra seconds to allow the water to lap lightly on them.

I was about to take a step towards the beach volleyball game when something hammered into my right leg. Whatever it was, it nearly knocked me off my feet. I knew there was no way it was a small fish or even a turtle. I felt the blow of whatever it was then several seconds later felt its tail flounder against my leg.

The other girls could tell something was wrong. Mia and Ann ran towards me, sprinting through the shallow water to see if I needed help.

"Presley, what happened?" asked Mia.

"I am not sure, but I think a giant fish just brushed my leg."

"Oh, that happens in the shallow water sometimes," said Ann.

"No! You don't understand. This was not a normal fish; it was huge!"

-19-

The three of us stood there for a couple minutes, scanning the nearby water for any type of movement.

"Well, whatever it is, it's gone now," said Mia.

"What kind of fish would be up in the shallows near the beach?" I asked dumbfounded. This was the most popular spot with hundreds of kids swimming and splashing.

"That is weird," said Ann.

We three walked back towards the volleyball court to continue our game. I couldn't get my mind off the fish. I even had a small scratch on my leg, that evidenced something big had hit my leg.

After volleyball, we all went back to our cabins for some down time. Some of the other girls took a midday nap. Mia, Ann and I sat on Ann's bottom bunk to plan.

"Okay, so I would say that archery or swimming is our best chance to score some points," said Ann as small pieces of licorice fell out of her mouth.

She added, "Remember we need to win at least one event, then catch the fish in order to knock Marsh off his high horse and claim victory for D Cabin."

The archery contest didn't start out well for us. Two of us completely missed the target on our first shot. A variety of point values had been designated for different spots on the target. Each girl was given five shots, so the eight girls in our cabin had a total of 40 shots. By the time our shots were up, two arrows were stuck in trees behind the archery range, and four arrows were missing.

"Well, maybe archery isn't going to be the one for us," said Mia.

On our way back to our cabin, we walked by the main registration area where a big wooden leader board sign had been posted. Written in bold white letters: B Cabin was in first place with 10 points.

The next day kickball tournament went a little better. We won our first two games but lost the third game to the girls in A Cabin. So far, our cabin was 0-2 in the competition, with only five events left. It also meant camp would end on Sunday.

The leader board was starting to get more and more visitors. B Cabin still led with 15 points. They had gotten third place in the kickball tournament. They might have won if Marsh hadn't lost his temper and whipped the ball at a kid on the other team. The kid juked and avoided the ball. The throw went rolling into the outfield as two runners jogged in, game over. But third place still gave them five additional points.

"Girls, tomorrow is the swimming competition. Any advice on and how we can win this one?" asked Miss Katie.

Most of the other girls in our cabin just looked around. The rules for the swimming competition were simple. Each cabin picked their three fastest swimmers, and they did a relay race on Lake David.

"We will do it," said Mia.

"We as in *us*?" I asked.

"We got this," Mia said trying to reassure me.

"Okay, then you three will represent D Cabin in today's swimming competition," said Miss Katie. The other girls in the cabin were relieved they didn't have to swim and compete in the swimming race.

We went back to our bunks for some reading time. I looked at Mia with an inquisitive stare.

"I know what you are thinking," she said.

"No, we don't have a chance of winning first place in the swimming contest. But we can use it to our advantage for something down the road," she said.

One thing about Mia was that she was always

planning our next move. The way she thought reminded me of a checkers or a chess game. One move was just a setup for her next move. She was a very strategic thinker.

Only when I found out her plan, I wasn't sure this was a good plan at all!

-20-

Mia laid out her plan for the swimming competition. This relay race required three swimmers to race individually to a buoy about 100 feet from the end of the dock, and then return to the dock to tag the next swimmer to go and so forth.

During the last week of camp, I had learned that Mia and Ann were both great swimmers. Both girls swam on their school swim team and loved the water.

But I didn't see myself as much of a swimmer. I was good in the water, but not sure I could help them in the race.

The counselors would keep track, and the top three teams competed in the final round.

Our first race was pitted against the boys from E Cabin. I was nervous and unsure of myself. I didn't want to let my cabin down…or Mia and Ann.

Mia could tell I was feeling anxious and walked over to me. "Listen to me, Presley; you got this. Ann and I believe in you. It's time you need to believe in yourself," she said.

I looked around, noticing most of the campers had stayed to watch the relay races. The weather was hot and humid with the temperature around 88 degrees. Many of the campers were swimming and playing on the beach, making the race even more chaotic.

Our team lined up at the end of the dock right next to the three swimmers from E Cabin.

The whistle blew, and Ann dove in off the creaky wooden dock. She disappeared, swimming quite a way under the water. I was scared at first when she didn't come up but could make out her silhouette just below the water. When her head finally popped up, she was in a perfect front swimming motion. She was fast and had quite a lead on the first boy. By the time she rounded the first buoy, she had an even bigger lead on him. She quickly closed the distance back to the dock tagging Mia.

Mia was even stronger in the water. I felt some relief watching her swim; I knew we had a huge lead. By the time, Mia got back to the dock, my confidence level was much higher. My body's adrenaline quickly kicked in as I vaulted as hard as I could off the dock into the crisp lake. When I crested to the top of the water, I swam with all my might towards the buoy. I felt fast. I don't know how fast I was really going, but I felt fast. I circled the buoy and crossed the finish line way ahead of the boy.

We won our first race, but was it enough to make it to the finals? After all, there were 14 teams. *Did we have a fast enough time to make the final three?*

-21-

Our cabin stayed and watched the other cabins race. It was exciting, and we always cheered loudest when the girls team took on any boys' team. There were some really fast swimmers. The last heat paired up boys from M and B Cabin. I recognized the three swimmers for B Cabin, and of course, Marsh was the last leg.

The whistle blew, and the boys took off like torpedoes. Both swimmers were neck and neck around the buoy. By the time they reached the dock, it looked like a tie. The second boys took off, and they were both fast, staying within inches of each other.

That would all change when the last leg started.

Marsh hit the water effortlessly, reminding me of a dolphin jumping waves in the ocean. There was no wasted movement. The speed he swam at was unbelievable. The tied race quickly got out of hand as Marsh ran away with the win. The entire crowd of boys cheered as Marsh swam past the finish line.

He glanced back towards the other boy, who was now trailing way behind him and laughed.

No doubt they would be one of the final three teams in the championship race.

The teams waited breathlessly as the counselors recorded and compared the times of all the cabins. After ten minutes, they blew their whistle, and the teams huddled around for the results.

"Great swimming today everyone," said the counselor. "The three cabins in the final are H, B and D!"

When they announced our cabin, all the girl campers started cheering like crazy. One girls' team was in the swimming competition!

"Girls, all we have to do is beat one of those

two teams. We only need to earn eight points," explained Mia. "With the eight points and then the forty for catching Big Lou, we can still win the golden arrow contest."

While our objective was a stretch, there was still a small glimmer of hope for D Cabin. I wanted to win badly—not just for us but for all the girls at camp. I also wanted to win for all the other campers who had been tormented by Marsh and the boys of B Cabin.

"Mia, both those teams are really fast," said Ann.

"They are, but so are we. We have to beat one team and get some points," she assured us.

The mid-July sun was baking my skin as we waited at the end of the dock. I was hoping that some of the other campers would have gotten bored with waiting around and had left. Unfortunately, no one left; in fact, minute by minute, it seemed more people were coming to see the final race.

The nearby beaches were jammed with campers, counselors and other spectators.

The boys of H Cabin were going to win; there was no doubt about it. All three of their boys were city champion swimmers.

We had to beat Marsh and B Cabin. Looking ahead, we knew the swimming competition was our best chance at getting points.

The three teams lined up and readied themselves at the end of the dock. Marsh occasionally glanced at us, smirking.

In his mind, they had already won second place. We were just there for his benefit to embarrass.

The crowd began to grow restless and get loud as they lined us up in order. The final race was a little longer as the buoy had been moved about fifty feet past its previous spot.

The loud whistle snapped with an authority as Ann dove in. The crowd roared as the H Cabin boys shot out to a big lead. But Ann was neck and neck with the B Cabin swimmer. They both rushed past the marker and turned for a return sprint back to the dock.

The H Cabin boys second swimmer was in the water well ahead of everyone else. Ann tapped the dock, and Mia rocketed into the water with a subtle but powerful splash.

By the time she surfaced, she was about ten feet in front of the B Cabin swimmer. While the other boy was struggling, Mia was finding her rhythm, distancing herself even more from him. She crossed the buoy and was heading back towards me with a sizable lead.

I turned towards Marsh who looked calm and ready. I steadied myself, and as soon as Mia tapped the dock, I dove in.

The water rushed over my body, and I felt strong as I surfaced. My arms and legs were working in perfect unison.

I rounded the marker and saw Marsh out of the corner of my eye. He had made up a lot of ground and was catching up.

The big lead that I had was gone. We were both in a dead sprint to the dock.

When we were 50 yards away, I watched in disbelief as Marsh zoomed past me.

I had lost the lead, and it looked like our chance to win the competition was gone.

-22-

I didn't slow but watched as Marsh pulled farther and farther ahead. The crowd erupted as we
drew closer and closer to the finish.

Then something strange happened...

Marsh stopped and went under the water. I slowed
to see if he needed help, but he quickly popped back
up. Noticing he wasn't crying out, I kept swimming.
A late sudden burst of adrenaline kicked in as I
closed in closer to the finish line. The girl campers
were standing up, cheering and yelling.

I tapped the dock well ahead of Marsh as Mia
and Ann jumped in the water next to me. They
started hugging me and celebrating.

Seconds later Marsh finished touching the deck defeated. I saw him mouthing something to the counselor in charge. Whatever he was saying, he didn't look happy.

"What happened? Why did he stop?" I asked.

"I don't know. He started yelling something, looked around and diving back down into the water. The whole thing looked weird from the dock," said Ann.

"Way to go, D Cabin!" yelled Miss Katie as she sprinted down the dock. "We are on the leader board, ladies!" she added.

Her excitement made me smile even bigger. The three of us walked up onto the beach, only to be mobbed by a host of the other female campers.

And we beat Marsh at something at camp.

Not everyone was happy for us, however. Marsh was still arguing and pleading his case to a host of counselors. His face was bright red, and he was mad.

Mia noticed I was looking at him. "Press, stop! Don't worry about him. We won," she said.

We walked back to the cabin, giggling and laughing—proud of our rare accomplishment. The eight second place points put our cabin on the leader board and gave us a chance.

After drying off and changing, I heard loud clattering of the front screen door. Miss Katie skipped in a with a big grin. She walked towards us in excitement.

"I am so proud of you girls!" she said yelling.

"Hey, what was up with Marsh? Why did he stop?" I asked.

"You know Marsh. He just has to win. I think he got tired and overdid himself. But he claims he hit something big—really big in the water," said Miss Katie.

"Like a log or something?" I asked.

"No, he is convinced it was a fish. It was probably a log or a turtle," she said. "But I think he is just making excuses. The chances of a big fish being anywhere around the swimming area is almost impossible."

The judges also thought he was making excuses and didn't believe him. They counted the race as official, and the boys of B Cabin came in third place. The best part was they got beat by a trio of girls!

-23-

I learned a valuable lesson that day. We had stood up to the bully without being negative or rude. This felt better than revenge. After the prank war, I was always worried about making Marsh pay or what he would do to us. We were always looking over our shoulders, which isn't a good feeling. Beating him fair and square was the right way to vanquish him, and it felt amazing.

Now we just had to figure out a way to catch Big Lou.

"Hungry?" Ann asked, hanging a gummy worm down the railing of Mia's top bunk. It was red and blue—my favorite one.

We chomped on the gummy worms, reflecting

on the exciting week. Only four days remained of camp. I tried not to think about it because the thought made me sad. I missed my parents, but I felt a freedom and independence at camp.

I also had friends—real friends—the ones that you can really talk to and not worry about being judged. I looked at myself differently. I was tan, and my blonde hair was brighter from spending so much time outdoors at camp. Even deeper than that, when I looked at myself in the mirror, I was happy with who I saw looking back at me. This was the first time in my life that I felt that way.

"Tomorrow is the basketball game and Friday the two-mile run. Let's be honest, we don't have a shot at either one of them. Saturday is dodgeball, and yep, we're not going to win that one either," said Mia.

"Just like our original plan, we have to catch Big Lou on Sunday," said Ann.

"Girls, I love it! We have already done more than I ever thought was possible. Beating those boys will be one of the greatest camp memories I will ever have," I said.

I added, "But you both know the chance of catching Big Lou is slim. No one has caught that fish since the day it was released ten years ago."

Camp had already changed my life. *Did we have to catch Big Lou for it be a success?* No, but it would put an exclamation point on our time at Camp Golden Arrow.

"Umm, Press, I don't think that's true," said Ann.

"What part?" I replied.

"The part about no one ever seeing that fish again," said Ann.

"Those are just crazy campfire stories that kids tell at camp. There are literally hundreds of fabricated or made-up stories about Big Lou," said Mia.

"True, but I heard one last week that I think we should check into," said Ann.

She added, "We need to talk to Bernie."

-24-

Bernie Edwards was a huge part of Camp Golden Arrow. He and his wife Elaine had started volunteering at camp shortly after they had retired. Before retirement, Bernie was an elementary custodian, and Elaine was a school librarian. No one knew how old they really were, but they had gotten an award for thirty years of service at camp.

They spent their summers in a small cabin on the outskirts of Camp Golden Arrow. They worked for free and enjoyed every second of summer camp, especially helping kids. Elaine ran the camp library and taught craft lessons. Bernie was the head of maintenance. He was often seen riding around on the golf cart or lawn mower. He took great pride in the camp and did his best to keep it looking clean.

Bernie also liked to tell stories. His favorite pastime was telling campfire ghost stories. Bernie was the man who had told the ghost story about the man with one hand the first night we were here. While I didn't know his name at the time, I had seen Bernie every day at camp.

"What does Bernie have to do with finding Big Lou?" I asked.

"He was there the day Big Lou was released into David Lake," said Ann.

"Yeah, so were a lot of other counselors and camp employees," said Mia.

"No, Bernie was right there; he helped release the fish," explained Ann.

She added, "Plus I heard him talking about the fish before to some of the other counselors. They just blew him off, but he mentioned something about various fish sightings around the lake."

We started walking around camp, looking and

listening for any sign of Bernie. As we approached the camp store, we heard a loud buzz of a lawn mower off in the distance near the baseball fields.

It was Bernie, sporting his red bucket hat and Camp Golden Arrow t-shirt. We motioned for him to come over.

Slightly annoyed at being interrupted, he turned off the mower blades and drove the mower to our location.

"Girls, I am on tight schedule today. Mr. Creed wants the dodgeball field cut and marked out by the end of the day," said Bernie. Still, he shut off the mower and propped his feet on the dash.

"We were wondering if you could tell us about Big Lou?" asked Mia.

"Big Lou…" he said with a series of belly laughs. "What about him?" he added.

"We heard you were there when he was released," I said.

Bernie looked impressed, his shoulders straightened, and his chest stuck out a little farther than before. "You heard right; I was there. Boy, that is a fish! We put him in right on the beach, just off the north side of the dock."

He added, "At the time, the fish was pushing 70 pounds. He was a big blue catfish—biggest one I had ever seen."

"Have you ever seen him since?" I asked.

"I have, but no one believes me," he responded as his voice lowered.

"We believe you," said Mia.

Bernie perked back up. "About five years ago I was getting the dock ready for camp. No one else was here; it was late May. I was in the water repairing one of the dock legs when I felt something hit my leg. At first, I thought it was a piece of the dock, but it wasn't," he said.

"Big Lou?" I asked.

"Well, it was only for a second, and the water was murky, but I could have sworn I saw the flash of the yellow tag on the under belly of a fish," he declared.

"That's it? Any other time?" I asked.

"Nope, that's it," he said.

No one was around or on the lake more than Bernie. In all that time, he had only one encounter with Big Lou.

"For all we know, Big Lou could be dead by now," said Mia.

"No, he isn't dead. There have been a lot of reports about that fish every year at camp. A shadow here, a broken fishing line—strange stuff that can only be Big Lou," said Bernie.

"How do you know that it's Big Lou?" I quickly asked.

"I just do," he said. "He is out there waiting for the right person to hook into him."

"Thanks, Bernie," said Mia. With that, the three of us turned and started walking back towards the main camp area.

Bernie fired up the lawn mower, but we noticed he shut it off a couple of seconds later. I turned back to see Bernie standing up on top of the mower.

"If you girls have any chance of catching that fish, be unique. Try something unusual," advised Bernie before he sat back down and went back to his mowing.

I wondered, *Be unique?*

-25-

"What does that mean?" I finally asked.

"Who knows? I have no idea," said Mia.

We walked back quietly thinking about what Bernie had told us.

Walking by the camp store, Ann stopped us.

"Look," she said pointing to the glass window. There was a big sign selling night crawlers, minnows and frogs for fishing on Lake David. During the summer, fishing was so popular during camp, the store often sold out of the common bait having to reorder more from the city. The lake was full of fish, and it was easy to catch something.

"That's it…Bernie was right; that's the secret to catching Big Lou," said Ann.

Mia and I both stood there, wondering what Ann was talking about. Ann fished all the time. Every night and usually first thing in the morning, she had a line out in the lake.

"Girls, think about it. Big Lou is so big and old. He rules Lake David. So many kids have been using these same baits. A fish like Big Lou is looking for something different—unique," said Ann.

"Unique, like what?" I asked.

"That part, I don't know for sure, but the usual worms and lures won't work if we have any chance at catching Big Lou," said Ann as she munched on a piece of licorice.

My mind was racing, thinking of all kinds of ideas to try to use to lure Big Lou to our hook. We talked on the way back to our cabin. Hot dogs, sausage and some secret meat from the cafeteria all came up in conversation, but none really sparked Ann's attention.

"No, those won't work," Ann said.

"How do you know?" asked Mia.

"I don't know how to explain it, but somehow I just know," Ann contended.

The next two days flew by. We lost our first game in the basketball tournament. We played some girls who played travel basketball and were really good. They even gave the boys from B Cabin a decent game. But in the end, Marsh and his sweet jump shot gave his cabin ten more points and a first-place victory. B Cabin was really starting to rack up the points; it looked like they were well on their way to claiming their third camp trophy in a row.

Friday was the two-mile run. I thought we would have a chance to place in the race. A girl in our cabin named Allison who was a cross country runner was chosen to compete. She ran great but finished in fifth place—just out of reach of getting any points. A girl named Gracy was an amazing runner who beat everyone and ran away with first place. The only good thing that came out of the run was B Cabin placed tenth.

Ann was really doing her research. She was fishing all around the lake, trying to get a feel for where the huge catfish might be.

The three of us had spent a lot of time on the lake, looking for great fishing holes. I had fallen in love with fishing. I found it peaceful and loved the feel of reeling in a fish. Once I had caught a couple nice bass and catfish, I was hooked. It seemed like everywhere we went, other campers were there fishing. The fish on Camp David were high pressured and seemed to get a heavy diet of campers' worms and bait.

I was anxious for the fishing tournament, but also reluctant since it was going to be our last day at camp. I had grown so close to Mia and Ann. The only positive I could find about the situation was knowing we would remain close. There was no doubt that I would be coming back to Camp Golden Arrow next year and every year after. We even talked about all being counselors together someday.

Saturday morning was a big day around camp. It was time for the annual dodgeball game, and we had a lot of free time. We were allowed to go to the beach, fish, swim or just chill with friends. There had been a lot of structured events at camp and a very tight schedule.

Having the entire day to do what we wanted was exciting. Our plan was to watch the dodgeball tournament and then spend midday at the beach swimming.

-26-

Breakfast was a grand event to kick off our super Saturday morning. This was the biggest and best food I had since arriving at camp. There was an omelet bar, fresh fruit, biscuits and gravy and anything else you could dream about.

The boy cabins were really excited about the dodgeball tournament, but the girl cabin not so much. Our team was already planning on being out after the first game.

After breakfast, we headed towards the field. Bernie had cut and painted them to perfection. He sat overlooking the field on his lawn mower, watching as the campers enjoyed his handiwork. He waved to us when we saw us watching.

Spot on with their prediction, our cabin was out after the first game. The boys were so aggressive and took no mercy on our cabin. We watched as Marsh nailed our girls with the ball. The B Cabin boys were whipping the dodgeballs and flying around the field. The girls in our cabin tried their best but were no match for them. I was thankful the three of us weren't picked for the dodgeball game.

There was no doubt B Cabin would win and earn another 10 points for a first-place finish.

"Well, it looks like the B Cabin boys are going to have 45 points total for the week. This was more than enough to win as the second-place team from A Cabin had 30 points. We were in eleventh place out of the fourteen cabins, with eight points from our second-place swimming win.

"Just like I said, if we catch Big Lou, we win," said Ann.

Catching Big Lou was worth 40 points. In all reality, it could have been worth 1,000 points. Catching the catfish was like chasing a unicorn or finding gold at the end of the rainbow.

"Ann, what's the plan for tomorrow?" I asked.

"Catch Big Lou—same plan we have had since the first day of camp," repeated Ann.

"Ann, *that* is everyone's plan for tomorrow," Mia replied.

"I am sure it is, but *we* aren't like everyone else," she declared.

Most campers fished the north side of Lake David, which was much more remote with readily available bait fish. Anyone fishing there was sure to catch a lot of fish and some big ones too. The north side was the most likely spot for a fish like Big Lou to live.

But that wasn't where Big Lou would be.

"That's too easy, if he was near the north shore of David Lake, he would have been caught years ago," explained Ann.

"Okay…then, where…where is it that Big Lou lives?" I asked.

"That I don't know yet, but I can tell you it's not going to be the north shore or anywhere else where all these kids have been fishing," said Ann.

"Ann, we are running out of time," said Mia.

"Are we? The contest doesn't start until tomorrow. It would have been a shame if we had hooked into Big Lou before Sunday," she said confidently.

As we left the dodgeball games, Bernie saw us and motioned for us to stop. He had something to tell us—something important—but we didn't see him. Our minds were somewhere else.

-27-

Saturday night's bonfire party had a totally different feeling than the last one we had attended. Instead of excitement, there was a sense of loss; camp was coming to an end, and we would be saying goodbye the next afternoon.

The fishing contest ended officially at noon, and with it signaled the end of Camp Golden Arrow. Our parents were scheduled to be there from 12:30 to 1:00 p.m. to pick us up. The thought of returning to the city made me nauseous. Camp had taught me so much, but the greatest lessons I had learned were about myself.

I was 13 days without touching my cell phone or even thinking about it. My mind was clear, and I finally understood what my parents had been trying to tell me. They always said I was missing out on so much by being on my phone all the time.

I giggled to myself. *I bet all my social media connections think I was abducted by aliens or something!* It seemed like I was much more aware of the time I had wasted scrolling on my phone, waiting for people to like or comment on a picture. When I did get home, I knew I would never feel dependent on social media or my cell phone. I had a million fabulous pictures in my mind from all the memories at camp.

I now had something my cell phone could never give me. Having self-confidence was a new concept to me, but I was starting to like it.

The three of us sat around the big campfire in the middle of camp with all the other campers. There were camp songs and snacks. The night was muggy, but a quiet, cool wind tickled my hair, giving just enough relief from the heat. It was the perfect night.

I looked towards the open fields and saw the ambient lights of thousands of fireflies. They danced across the horizon reminding me of the city.

I laid down on our blanket and looked up at the night sky. There wasn't a cloud in the sky. The stars were bright and numbered in the millions.

Wow!

Camp Golden Arrow was a blessing—a moment in time that I knew would change my life forever in a positive way.

Mia nudged me. "Look, there is the North Star."

We had learned all about the stars and constellations in one of camp classes this week. I knew how to find the Big and Little Dipper among other constellations.

Our star gazing was interrupted when a loud commotion started behind us. Turning to look, we saw Marsh dancing around, singing and joking.

"Just call us the three-time golden arrow champs," he was yelling. The boys were close enough that we could hear their conversations.

They were all bragging about how B Cabin had already won and that the fishing contest was just for fun. They had such a huge lead—even if another cabin caught the biggest fish, they couldn't beat B Cabin.

Unless someone caught Big Lou...

-28-

"Marsh, what if someone gets lucky and catches that fish?" asked one of the boys. It seemed like at least one rational boy still remained in B Cabin.

"Robbie, get real. You know that no one is catching Big Lou. I guarantee that fish doesn't even exist. Even if he did, he is dead by now. The trophy is as good as ours," Marsh said confidently as he strutted around. The other boys nodded in unison.

We sat listening to the boys brag; they were clueless that we were there. Or they just didn't care. Once we stopped messing with Marsh, he had grown bored with the girls of D Cabin.

Towards the end of the night, I noticed Bernie walking around the crowd of kids. It looked like he was on a mission, looking for someone.

He approached Miss Katie, talked to her, and she pointed in our direction. Bernie strolled towards us yelling something and waving his arms.

Not sure what he meant, we waved back. "Maybe he was saying goodbye," said Mia.

As he came closer, his excitement was obvious to everyone, including the boys of B Cabin.

"Girls, girls! I think I might have more information for you on how to find Big Lou," he yelled.

My heart stopped as I watched Marsh stop in mid-sentence and turn to face Bernie. He had heard the old man's rant, and now he was extremely interested in his conversation with us.

"Gals, I have something for you," said Bernie excitedly. I could see Marsh out of the corner of my eye eavesdropping but trying not to make it obvious. Ann saw him too.

"Bernie...Bernie! Can you talk a little quieter please?" Ann begged.

"I wanted to give you girls something," he said, slipping a piece of paper in my right hand. I quickly put it in my pocket, hoping Marsh had not seen the handoff.

"Thanks, but what is it?" Ann asked.

"I think it will help you find the fish—or at least give you a good starting spot to start fishing in the morning," he said.

Then as quickly as he had arrived, Bernie was dancing his way through the crowd of kids towards the s'mores bar on one of the picnic tables.

I knew it was too late. Marsh had heard most of the conversation and was walking in our direction. I quickly removed the paper from my pocket and bent down to pretend I was tying my shoe while shoving the paper in my sock.

"What was that old man talking to you guys about?" Marsh demanded.

"You know Bernie; he is always talking about something," Ann said quickly.

"Quit playing with me!" Marsh ordered sharply. "I heard him say something about Big Lou. I thought I saw him hand you something."

He walked closer to me. "Empty your pockets," he growled.

"She doesn't have to listen to you," Mia said.

"No, it's okay, Mia. I put both hands in my pockets and showed him they were totally empty.

Just then I heard Miss Katie's voice.

"D Cabin, let's roll; it's almost lights-out time," she called.

Unsure of his next move, Marsh stood staring.

"Good luck tomorrow," Ann said with a grin.

Miss Katie shot Marsh a look that caused the boy to return to his friends.

"Let's go girls, tomorrow is going to be here before you know it. You have a fish to catch," encouraged Miss Katie with a wink.

-29-

We were careful not to say anything until we got back to our cabin.

"I talked to Bernie," said Miss Katie, making it obvious how she knew about the fish.

We went over to the desk and turned on the lamp. I reached down and pulled the paper from my sock that Bernie had handed me.

He had given us a map of David Lake. On the map were small circles and dates. The circles were all over the map.

"How is this going to help us?" asked Mia.

"I don't know. We just need to study it. The answer to finding Big Lou is here, or Bernie wouldn't have given it to us," replied Ann.

There seemed to be no pattern to the sightings on the map. The girls counted a total of 20 circles, and they were everywhere—from the south side inlet to the northern shore of the lake.

"How do we know these were even real sightings of Big Lou?" I asked.

"They don't have to all be Big Lou, but some of them are for sure," said Ann.

"Well, good luck, girls. I am going to round up the rest of the girls and get them back to the cabin," said Miss Katie.

The three of us stared at that map for another hour. The other girls returned, oblivious to our adventure. They were too worried about talking about cute boys and their hair.

Ann was starting to get frustrated.

"It's not your fault; it was a long shot anyway," I said.

"I know but…" Ann said, chomping on a gummy worm.

Mia suddenly jumped in.

"Look at this!" she exclaimed as she held up a piece of scrap paper she had been scribbling on.

She had all the dates written down with circles around all the June dates over the last several years. There were a total of four June sightings.

"I still don't see it," I said.

"I do!" said Ann excitedly. She grabbed Mia's paper and circled the same dates on the map.

"This is where Big Lou will be tomorrow," she stated confidently as she drew a big circle over David Lake.

"You can't be serious," I said.

"It makes perfect sense," said Mia.

-30-

"Press, go grab your cell phone," said Ann.

Puzzled, I walked over to my suitcase and powered it on.

"You know I don't have any signal," I said.

"Set your alarm for 5:30 a.m.," she said.

She added, "I have a plan, but we will need to start early."

My phone powered up and buzzed to life. It had a lot of battery left since I hadn't turned it on since I had arrived at Camp Golden Arrow.

"Lights out, girls," Miss Katie said as she switched off the main cabin light.

"Miss Katie, can you come here? I need you to do us a huge favor," said Ann.

Katie flipped the light back on and walked over towards us.

"Sure! What's up?" she asked.

"I need you to go talk to Jeff and talk rather loudly," I said.

Jeff was the main counselor from B Cabin, and he and Katie attended the same high school. They were pretty good friends, so it wouldn't be abnormal for her to talk to him.

"Okay, what should I say?" she asked.

"Small talk at first…but act excited. When he asks why, let him know that some of the girls know where Big Lou is. Oh, and remember to talk very loud," added Ann.

"Okay, is that it?" she asked.

"One more thing…make sure he knows we are getting up early. Tell him we want to get a jump on our secret spot ahead of the other campers. Say we are leaving to go fishing around 5:30 a.m.," Ann finished.

Miss Katie nodded in agreement. She was cool.

She could have asked us a million questions, but she didn't. She knew we had a plan and trusted us.

Miss Katie left and headed towards B Cabin. The three of us waited anxiously for her return. She was gone about ten minutes, but if felt like two hours.

She was humming our favorite camp song as she returned to the cabin.

"Mission complete," she said as she entered the cabin.

"Did you remember to say everything?" asked Mia.

"Yep, every word," she said.

"Did Jeff seem interested?" Ann asked.

"Not really, he seemed more annoyed…like why I was bothering him about a fish this late at night." She chuckled then quickly added, "But someone in the cabin was really interested. He heard every word."

-31-

Ann walked over and whispered something into one of the other girl's ears who was lying down on the bottom bunk next to us. She perked up and then nodded yes before closing her eyes and going back to sleep.

"The stage has been set, girls; let's try to sleep," said Mia.

I laid down and closed my eyes. I was tired, and the sun had taken a toll on me. Within seconds I was out.

The annoying sound of my alarm startled me awake. I woke up dazed and confused. It had been weeks since I had used any alarm, and we usually woke up around 6:30 a.m., so the hour earlier threw me off. I wiped my eyes, trying to remember where I was and if I was still dreaming.

"Press, let's go! We need to go," encouraged Mia, standing by the back door. I squinted, making out two shadows holding fishing poles in the open doorway. They both had pulled up their hoods and were ready to go. I jumped up and threw on a hoodie and grabbed my pole.

"We have to move fast; it will take us a good hour to get to Parker's Ridge on the west side of the lake," said Mia.

I nodded in agreement. I knew that hike well. We often traveled to Parker's Ridge and fished throughout the week. That isolated spot was a perfect spot for a giant catfish.

"Here, turn these on, and make sure they stay on," Mia said, handing me a big flashlight.

We exited the back of the cabin and started walking quickly toward the edge of the lake. Our three lights could be seen from a mile away, and that's exactly what we wanted. There wasn't a camper crazy enough to go out in the dark without a flashlight around Lake David.

The three of us walked at a furious pace for about 30 minutes before Mia stopped. "Listen…" she whispered.

We stopped and stood still. After a couple of seconds, we could hear noise behind us. We could make out the faint outline of lights. Four flashlights were in close pursuit about a hundred yards behind us. The illumination of the flashlights made them easy to pick out still in the predawn. The sun was starting to rise as we kept our lights on while heading towards the fishing spot.

"Perfect! Let's keep moving," said Mia.

By the time we arrived at our fishing spot, the sun had started to rise. It was a perfect time to fish—a perfect time to catch Big Lou. We were sure the giant catfish would be patrolling, looking for an early morning breakfast.

It took us about an hour to arrive at Parker's Ridge right on time as planned. We walked down the ridge to the waterfront where there was a flat area perfect for fishing. We spread out and started casting into the lake. Within minutes, the woods erupted with noise as birds scattered from the nearby trees. Four objects materialized out from the ridge and walked down to our fishing area.

"What's up, girls? You didn't think we would let you three come out in the dangerous, dark woods by yourself," Marshall said, laughing. "I guess since we are here, we might as well fish too."

They wanted to catch the legendary fish, but if they didn't, they for sure didn't want us to catch it. The thought of his losing to the girls from D Cabin had to be unbearable for Marsh.

After a couple of minutes of no bites, Marsh started to get antsy.

By now the sun was up and bright.

"You thought you were going to sneak one by the old Marsh man, huh?" he mocked as he looked towards the girls.

The three of us turned toward him, pulling back

our hoods. It took him a second, but he suddenly noticed something wasn't right—he saw only one of the twins.

"Who's this? Where's your sister?" he snarled. His confusion at only seeing Mia was unsettling.

-32-

Standing near Parker's Ridge were three girls from D Cabin—Mia, Sammy, one of the other girls from our cabin, and me. Sammy had agreed to help the night before.

"Oh, sorry, Marsh. Miss Katie was telling the truth; we did find out where to catch Big Lou. But as you can see, it's not here," Mia said smugly.

Marsh turned to his crew. "Boys, we got to go! The other sister is the one who is going to catch Big Lou." The boys took off running back towards the camp.

The night before when we outlined the perfect plan with decoys, we knew Marsh would be watching us that morning. Sammy was about the same height as Ann, so she made a perfect body double. We were hoping an hour was enough time to distract Marsh and keep him away from the camp. It would take him less time to get back, but his return wouldn't be quick.

Our only hope was that we had delayed him long enough for Ann to catch Big Lou.

We had pinpointed Big Lou's location, and it wasn't anywhere near Parker's Ridge. Ann had a much shorter walk.

Last night while looking at Bernie's map, Ann had noticed something peculiar about the June sightings of Big Lou.

As we had studied the map, a pattern did appear. The first group of sightings four years ago had been on the south end. Three years ago, Big Lou had been sighted on the west end. Last year the circles appeared on the north end near Parker's Ridge. The big fish was moving clockwise all summer around the lake, devouring every baitfish and frog in its path.

There was only one unique spot—two circles with dates from this year's camp on the map. And those two circles were in the one spot no one would ever have thought a huge catfish would live. One circle was near the dock, and the other was on Beaumont Beach—the same beach where we swam and splashed in every day.

Beaumont Beach was the one spot that never got fished. That was all changing this morning.

Ann had a line in the water ten minutes after we had cleared the woods heading to Parker's Ridge. Ann was alone with Big Lou.

She had waded out to her knees in the cool lake waters. Behind her was the sandy beach and to her left was our cabin. Bernie had not only given us a good place to start fishing for Big Lou, he also given us an idea of what bait to use to catch the fish.

We were already sure that Big Lou had the luxury of feasting on every kind of lure and worm around David Lake. Tricking that old fish was going to take something special.

As we jogged back towards the beach, my heart raced. Our return pace was much faster but maneuvering through the thick shoreline was still difficult.

Did Ann find Big Lou?

Did Marsh make it back in time to ruin our chances again?

-33-

"What's all that noise?" Mia asked, stopping us from running.

We stood and listened. We couldn't see the camp yet but were close. Something was happening for sure.

"I hear it too! Let's go!" I said, picking up our pace even faster.

Minutes later we cleared the last hill and could see Beaumont Beach…and what a sight it was!

I glanced at my watch, and it was about 7:30 a.m. A huge crowd had gathered near the shallow waters. We sprinted the rest of the way before stopping right outside the huge crowd. Every camper and counselor seemed to be there.

We had to weave our way through the crowd before finally catching sight of Ann…standing in the water with Miss Katie. When they saw us, they gestured for us to join them. I noticed Ann had her hand in the water.

"Girls, I need your help," she said.

We walked over and could see she had a hold of a fish. The three of us positioned ourselves next to her and Miss Katie.

"Be careful; he is big. Don't touch the dorsal or the pectoral fins. You might get poked," she instructed.

We slowly reached into the water, carefully feeling for the belly of the fish.

"Okay, on the count of three," said Ann, seeing we were ready to pick up the giant catfish.

"One, two, three!" she said.

We lifted with all our might and could feel the huge fish slowly rising out of the water. I almost lost my grip and fell over when I saw Big Lou!

It took all of us to lift the fish out of the water,

but when we did, the crowd went crazy. Cameras started going off, and people were cheering.

Big Lou was all that had been advertised!

The fish was over four feet long and weighed over 100 pounds. The same yellow tag that had been put on by the conservation officer so many years ago was still on Big Lou!

I scanned the crowd and saw Bernie smiling. I knew he was proud of us. Then my eyes met Marsh. He wasn't as happy as everyone else. The look on his face was a mix of amazement and jealousy.

The look on Ann's face was priceless. She was holding the head of Big Lou. We quickly took more pictures of the fish.

Ann carefully removed the hook, and with great respect, we lowered Big Lou back into the water. The fish looked like a giant submarine as it slowly swam back into the depths of David Lake. We three would only be a small part in the history and legend of Big Lou.

But we would be written into its history.

The crowd started to divide in the middle as Mr. Creed made his way towards the beach. He stood at the foot of beach and held up a big, bold golden trophy.

"Congratulations to the girls of D Cabin, this year's winner of the golden trophy award," said Mr. Creed. The girls from our cabin joined us as we ran up to the beach. We were the champions of the summer at Camp Golden Arrow.

After a couple minutes, the crowd slowly started to disperse. Some kids still wanted to go fishing one last time that summer on David Lake. While catching Big Lou was the ultimate prize, fishing was still a favorite pastime at the camp.

After getting cleaned up, we returned to our cabin. Not much time was left, and the excitement of the morning was wearing off as we started to prepare ourselves to say goodbye. Mia and Ann had become my best friends.

"Girls, I have to tell you thank you," I started.

"Press, you are our best friend," said Mia.

"We are going to have you come stay this summer at our farm. And we will write to each other all the time," added Ann.

Camp had taught me so many lessons. I was leaving so much happier than I had been. The last two weeks were the greatest of my life.

Our bags were packed, and we were getting ready to leave D Cabin when we heard a knock on the back door. Standing in the doorway was Marsh.

I walked over and opened the door. I could tell he had no plans on coming in the cabin.

"I just wanted to tell you girls, nice job catching Big Lou."

"Thanks," we replied in unison.

Then he walked away. I figured that was as close as we would get to an apology.

The three of us walked down the trail towards the main camp cabin. We passed the store, the cafeteria and all the special places that made camp. As we walked, campers would yell out congratulations and kind words.

We were camp rock stars, and we knew it.

"Just wait until next year…" Ann said.

Then camp was over. My parents were waiting for me, so I hugged Ann, Mia and Miss Katie. I fought back tears as I walked away from my new friends.

Before I knew it, I was back in my parents' car on the long dirt road, driving away from camp. I saw my reflection in the side window of the car, and this time I smiled. I was proud of what I saw. I was proud to be me. The search for Big Lou was more about the search for myself than anything else.

I wrote to Mia and Ann as soon as I got home. Five days later I received a letter from both of them. Inside was a newspaper clipping of us that had been the feature story on the front page of their local newspaper. The story told how we had caught the legendary Big Lou, and the accompanying full-color picture was huge!

The three of us and Miss Katie were smiling as we held the giant catfish in the shallow waters of

Beaumont Beach. Big Lou was posing perfect for the picture. I looked closer and could even see the hook in his mouth. Then I burst out laughing out loud.

There, attached to the hook was one of Ann's gummy worms…

About the Author

LANE WALKER is an award-winning author, speaker and educator. His book collection, Hometown Hunters, won a Bronze Medal at the Moonbeam Awards for Best Kids Series. In the fall of 2020, Lane launched another series called The Fishing Chronicles. Lane is an accomplished outdoor writer in the state of Michigan. He has been writing for the past 20 years and has over 250 articles professionally published. Walker has a real passion for outdoor recruitment and getting kids excited about reading. He is a former fifth grade teacher and elementary school principal. Currently, he is a Director/Principal at a technical center in Michigan. Walker is married with four, amazing children.

Find out more about the author at www.lanewalker.com.